Published in Canada by Tundra Books, a division of Random House of Canada Limited,
One Toronto Street, Suite 300, Toronto, Ontario M5C 2V6

Published in the United States by Tundra Books of Northern New York,
P.O. Box 1030, Plattsburgh, New York 12901

Library of Congress Control Number: 2012945430

Library and Archives Canada Cataloguing in Publication

Charles, Veronika Martenova
It's not about the tiny girl! / Veronika Martenova Charles ; illustrated
by David Parkins.

(Easy-to-read wonder tales)
Short stories based on Thumbelina and toads tales from around the world.
ISBN 978-1-77049-329-2. – ISBN 978-1-77049-334-6 (EPUB)

1. Fairy tales. I. Parkins, David II. Title. III. Series: Charles,
Veronika Martenova. Easy-to-read wonder tales.

PS8555.H4224Z1839 2013 jC813'.54 C2012-905306-6

We acknowledge the financial support of the Government of Canada through the
Canada Book Fund and that of the Government of Ontario through the Ontario Media
Development Corporation's Ontario Book Initiative. We further acknowledge the support of
the Canada Council for the Arts and the Ontario Arts Council for our publishing program.

**ONTARIO ARTS COUNCIL
CONSEIL DES ARTS DE L'ONTARIO**

Edited by Stacey Roderick

www.tundrabooks.com

Printed and bound in China

1 2 3 4 5 6   18 17 16 15 14 13

TUNDRA BOOKS

CONTENTS

SHOW AND TELL
PART 1

"Guess what I brought

for Show and Tell today,"

Lily said to Ben and Jake

at recess.

She took a walnut shell

from her pocket

and opened it.

Inside was a teeny, tiny doll,

lying on a piece of cotton.

"Can I see?" asked Ben.

"Wow. She's so little!"

"This is Thumbelina,"

Lily told her friends.

"Who's Thumbelina?" asked Jake.

"In the story, she is a tiny girl

who was born in a flower pot,"

explained Lily.

"She sleeps in a nutshell,

and some animals steal her.

Then a bird takes her away –"

"I know a story like that,"

interrupted Jake.

"But it's not about a tiny girl.

It's about a tiny boy!

Do you want to hear it?"

"Sure!" replied Lily and Ben.

PEANUT BOY

(*Thumbelina* from Chile)

In a mountain valley lived

a woman and her husband.

One day, the woman saw

an old man passing by.

"Is there some place where

I could get something to eat?"

he asked. "All I've had today

are some peanuts."

"Come in," said the woman,

inviting the man into her hut.

She gave him a plate of potatoes.

"Do you have any children?"

the old man asked.

"No, but we wish we did,"

the woman replied sadly.

"It's lonely with no children."

The old man finished eating.

He reached into his bag

and pulled out a peanut.

"Thank you for being so kind,"

the old man said.

"Plant this peanut

and you'll get your wish."

The woman laughed,

but later she planted the nut

and watched it sprout.

When its leaves turned yellow,

she pulled the plant out

and saw a pod in its roots.

She split it open.

What a surprise!

Inside was a tiny boy

the size of a peanut!

So the woman and her husband

named the baby Peanut.

They loved him and cared for him,

but in time they began to worry

because Peanut didn't grow.

Every time his parents went out,

they carried Peanut with them.

But once, they left him at home.

After a while, Peanut wandered

outside and climbed a stone.

Suddenly, it began to rain heavily.

Peanut hid among the leaves

of a fallen branch.

Just then, a huge bird came

looking for twigs for its nest.

It grabbed the branch

where Peanut was hiding!

The bird soared into the air.

Peanut clung to the leaves

as he was carried

high up to a mountaintop.

The bird dropped the branch

beside its nest and left.

Peanut crawled off the branch.

He looked for something to eat

and found some berries.

There was a hole in the rock

where he could sleep.

So Peanut stayed close to the nest,

watching when the bird

came back to feed her babies.

One day, he spied a snake

climbing up to the nest,

ready to strike and eat the chicks.

They hadn't learned to fly yet,

so they chirped desperately

when they saw the snake.

Peanut looked around

and saw a twig with thorns on it.

He picked it up, and when

the snake opened its mouth

to grab the chicks,

he pierced its long tongue

with the thorny twig.

The serpent pulled back in pain,

fell off the rock,

and tumbled down into the canyon.

Just then, the mother bird came

and saw how Peanut

had saved her chicks.

She left again and returned

with a big bone in her beak.

She placed it in front of Peanut.

This must be a bone of a giant,

thought Peanut, and he touched it.

At once, his body began to grow

until he was as big as a normal boy.

Then the bird tapped him

with her wing

and turned her head toward a trail.

She wants me to go with her,

thought Peanut.

How different everything
looked now!

He climbed down the steep trail,
following the bird all the way
to the bottom of the mountain.

There he saw a hut.

"I know this place!" cried Peanut.

"This is where my parents live!"

The mother bird circled above,

and then flew away.

When Peanut first entered the hut,

his parents didn't recognize him.

But after he told them his story,

they were happy to have him back

and amazed to see him fully grown.

★ ★ ★

"That's a good story," said Lily.

"What did you bring

for Show and Tell?" she asked Ben.

"I brought my pet rock,"

he replied, taking a rock out

of his coat pocket.

It had button eyes glued on it.

Ben poked at the eyes.

"This reminds me of another story,"

he said. "It's about a tiny boy

who fought ogres!"

"How could he fight them

if he was so small?" asked Jake.

"I'll tell you," said Ben.

★

LITTLE INCH

(*Thumbelina* from Japan)

There was once a man and a woman

who wished to have a child.

They went to a temple to pray.

"Please, give us a child," they said.

"We will love it even if it is

as small as the tip of a finger."

And soon after that

a baby boy was born to them,

as tiny as a fingertip.

They raised the boy with love

and care, but he didn't grow.

When he was one year old,

he was just one inch tall.

"Let's call him Little Inch,"

his parents decided.

When he was five years old,

the boy was *still* one inch tall.

And when he was seven,

still he was only one inch tall.

One day, Little Inch said,

"I want to go and see the world."

"You're too small," said Mother.

"There are ogres in the world.

Who will protect you?"

"I'll take your sewing needle,"

said Little Inch.

"I will defend myself with it."

"But how will you travel?"

Father asked. "You're too small."

"I'll use a rice bowl for a boat

and chopsticks to row with,"

Little Inch replied.

So his parents gave him

what he asked for.

They took him to the river

and set him afloat on the water.

"Good luck, Little Inch!"

his parents called as the river

carried the rice bowl away.

After many days,

Little Inch reached a big city.

He steered his rice bowl

to the shore and jumped out.

Then he walked around and

stopped in front of a grand house.

He went inside and called,

"Is anybody there?"

"Who's calling?"

asked the master of the house.

"Look down," said Little Inch,

who stood by a wooden shoe.

"Will you take me in?"

asked Little Inch.

"I can work for you."

"Well," replied the master,

"my daughter needs a playmate."

So Little Inch stayed

and played with the daughter.

One day, the girl went for a walk
and took Little Inch with her.
On the way home, two ogres
jumped out from behind the trees.
They grabbed her.

"Let her go!"

demanded Little Inch, and

he pulled out his needle-sword.

The ogres were amused.

One of them picked up Little Inch

and swallowed him whole.

But Little Inch could move

around in the ogre's stomach.

He waved his needle-sword,

stabbing the soft wall around him.

The ogre coughed

and spat Little Inch out.

Now the other ogre picked him up

and was about to crush him,

but Little Inch slipped

through the ogre's fingers

and jumped into his eye.

"Ouch!" the ogre screamed

and let go of the girl.

Then both ogres ran away,

back into the woods.

"Look! They dropped something!"

called Little Inch.

"This is a *magic* golden hammer,"

said the girl. "I've heard about it.

If I shake it,

my wish will come true."

"Please," asked Little Inch,

"can you wish to make me taller?"

The girl shook the hammer

and called, "Grow tall, grow tall!"

Instantly, Little Inch began

to grow until he was as tall

as the master's daughter.

"Thank you!" cried Little Inch.

In the years that followed,

Little Inch grew into

a fine young samurai.

Then he returned to his village

and cared for his parents

for the rest of their days.

★ ★ ★

"How did his parents

recognize him?" asked Jake.

"He could have been anyone."

"Well," said Ben,

"maybe he brought the rice bowl

they gave him."

"I know a story about a tiny boy, too,"

said Lily. "But he is bigger

than Peanut and Little Inch.

He is the size of a baby.

The story goes like this ..."

★

BABY-MAN

(*Thumbelina* from Native America)

On the shore of a beautiful lake

lived a little boy and his sister.

He didn't grow like other children

but remained small like a baby.

Yet, he was very, very strong

and could run faster

than the wind.

One winter day, Baby-man

said to his sister,

"Please make me a ball.

I'd like to go and play on the ice."

His sister made him a ball.

"Don't go too far!" she said.

Baby-man started off,

throwing the ball ahead of him

and running after it.

There were some dark spots

on the ice in the distance.

When Baby-man came closer,

he saw four large men

fishing with spears.

Baby-man threw the ball again,

and this time the ball landed

beside the men.

"Please," Baby-man called out,

"can you throw me the ball?"

The men turned around.

"Look at that little creature!"

they said with ugly laughs.

"Ready?" they asked the boy.

"Catch the ball!"

But they didn't toss it to him.

Instead, they passed it

among themselves

until the game bored them.

Then they dropped the ball

into the ice hole

and went back to their fishing.

How cruel! thought Baby-man.

They think because I'm small,

they can torment me.

Baby-man crept close to the men

and grabbed a large fish

they had just caught.

Then he ran away with it.

The men looked up.

First they thought that the fish

was running away by itself.

Then they realized it was

the boy carrying it.

"You'll pay for this!" they yelled.

They started running after him,

but the boy was too fast.

"Never mind," one of the men said.

"Tomorrow we'll follow his tracks

and kill him."

When Baby-man reached home,

he gave the fish to his sister.

"How did you get it?" she asked.

"I found it on the ice.

It's from our lake," he replied.

"But I think I have made

some men angry," he said.

The next morning, there was

a sound of snowshoes moving

across the frozen lake.

The sister went to the door

and saw four big men

coming toward the lodge.

"Brother!" she called, frightened.

"Some men are coming over here."

"Don't worry," Baby-man said.

He went outside and

waited for them by a boulder.

The men came onto the shore

and loaded their bows with arrows.

They climbed the hill to the lodge.

"I see the creature! Over there!"

one of the men called.

As they approached,

Baby-man pushed the boulder,

and it rolled toward them.

The men saw the boy do it

and jumped out of the way

just before the big stone

could crush them.

That is not an ordinary boy,

the men thought,

and they ran away in fear.

"Everything is all right now,"

Baby-man told his sister.

"Those men won't come back.

They're afraid of me," he said.

"Let's cut the fish up and dry it,"

the sister said.

"We will have enough to eat

for the whole spring."

SHOW AND TELL
PART 2

"Brrr!" said Jake.

"That story made me feel cold."

"What did you bring

for Show and Tell?" Ben asked.

"I forgot to bring something,"

Jake replied.

"I can lend you the nutshell,"

offered Lily.

"I'll show just Thumbelina."

"Thanks, Lily," said Jake.

"That's really nice of you!"

"But I need it back after school,"

Lily told Jake.

"Thumbelina needs her bed tonight."

The bell rang then,

calling the friends back to school.

★

ABOUT THE STORIES

Thumbelina, written by Hans Christian Andersen, is a well-known story about a tiny girl and her adventures. But there are many other stories about tiny characters, mainly boys, that can be found in cultures from around the world.

Peanut Boy is based on a story that comes from the Andes mountains in Chile, South America.

Little Inch is a retelling of a popular story from Japan called *Issun-boshi*. (A wish-fulfilling hammer is a favorite type of magical instrument in Japanese tales.)

Baby-man is inspired by part of a Native American tale, *Boy-Man*, that appeared in a collection titled *Indian Fairy Tales as Told to the Children of the Wiguam* by Mary Hazelton Wade, published in 1906.